PENGUIN YOUNG READERS LICENSES
An Imprint of Penguin Random House LLC

© 2017. All rights reserved. HATCHIMALS™ is a trademark of Spin Master Ltd., used under license. First published in the United Kingdom in 2017 by Puffin Books. Published in the United States in 2018 by Penguin Young Readers Licenses, an imprint of Penguin Random House LLC, 345 Hudson Street, New York, New York 10014. Printed in the USA.

Written by Kay Woodward
Illustrated by Lea Wade

ISBN 9781524788209   10 9 8 7 6 5 4 3 2 1

HATCHIMALS™
THE
GIGGLING
TREE

Penguin Young Readers Licenses
An Imprint of Penguin Random House

Contents

Mystery Eggs

"Ugh!" Ava threw her toy wand on the grass. It didn't matter how many times she waved it—not a single spark of magic appeared.

"Maybe you're doing it wrong?" said her younger brother, Oliver, who was dangling upside down from the tree swing nearby. "Have you tried saying abracadabra?"

"I've tried *everything*, Ollie," Ava said. "Nothing works."

Ever since she was old enough to read fairy tales, Ava had been absolutely certain that magic was real. She'd watched all the magicians' tricks she could find on the Internet. She'd studied how to track down fairies in the backyard. She'd read all about mythical beasts like unicorns and dragons. But she *still* hadn't found any signs of actual, real magic, and Ava couldn't help but feel a little disappointed.

Oliver flipped the right way up. "Maybe you just haven't looked in the right place yet." He jumped off the swing and grabbed for the lowest branch of the tree. Quickly, he started to climb. "How about up here?" he suggested with a grin.

"Oliver!" called Mom from behind the barbecue. "Not too high!" She flipped over a burger. "Besides, lunch will be ready soon."

Mystery Eggs

Dad poked his head out from the shed. He spotted Oliver and beamed at him. "Great climbing, Ollie!" he called. Then, on second thought: "I mean, be careful, and everything!"

Ava smiled. Mom and Dad were what their aunt Sophie called "eccentric." That meant they were a little strange, but in a cool sort of way. When Mom wasn't working in the city, and Dad wasn't fixing mountain bikes from home, they were always doing something new and exciting. Knowing Dad, he probably wanted to be up in the tree with Oliver.

"Hey!" called Oliver. "Look at me! I'm so high up, I'm almost in outer space!"

"Oliver . . . ," said Mom.

"Joking!" said Oliver. "Ava, come on. It's great up here. I haven't found any magic for you yet, but everything is really small when you're this high up. You look *tiny*!"

Ava grinned and waved at her

brother. She'd leave the tree climbing to Oliver—the swing was free now, so she could have her turn at last. Ava had a theory that if she swung high enough, she'd know what flying would feel like.

"Keep looking!" she called. "Magic hides in the most unlikely places. Or, at least, that's how it always works in books."

Soon Ava was swinging back and forth, her dark hair flying into her face and then streaming out behind

The Giggling Tree

her again. She wished that she could just wave a wand—one that actually worked—and it would make glittering silver wings appear on her back. Then she would soar up to join Oliver at the top of the tree, and they would fly up high into the clouds, where dragons and unicorns would . . . would . . .

Ava's daydream escaped her. She stared at the ground as it rose and fell beneath the swing, her mouth gaping.

What was that?!

"Whoa," she breathed. She wasn't sure exactly what she'd seen, but she knew that she had to investigate, and fast. She swung higher so that she was level with Oliver. "Look!" she called, pointing quickly with one hand.

Oliver followed her gaze, and his eyes widened. **"Whoa!"** he

exclaimed, echoing Ava.

"Come on!" yelled Ava. She swung down, stuck out her feet, and skidded to a halt, clouds of dirt billowing.

Oliver climbed down the tree a lot faster than he'd gone up it, landing in a heap at the bottom within just a few seconds. He sprang to his feet, shaking leaves from his brown hair.

"Did you *see* that?" gasped Ava.

Oliver nodded fast. "Let's go!" he said.

So they did. Except Ava sprinted

to the left . . . and Oliver ran to the right.

Typical Ollie, Ava thought. "You're going the wrong way!" she yelled over her shoulder, heading for the very spot she'd noticed from high up on the swing.

And there it was, nestled in a hollow at the magnolia tree's roots. It was white, and it was curved, and it was dotted with pink and teal speckles. Ava had never seen anything so beautiful. Or so *magical*.

Mystery Eggs

It was an egg.

She reached out and gently picked it up. The egg was smoother than silk and warm to the touch.

What could possibly be inside it? An eagle? A dodo? A little dragon?

She heard footsteps in the grass behind her. Ava spun around, moving to protect the egg, but it was just Oliver.

"Sis!" he called, his face lighting up. "What are you doing over here?" He didn't wait for an answer. "You should have gone to the rose bed! Because guess what I found! Actually, you won't guess. It's too awesome. Should I just tell you? I think I will. It's—"

Mystery Eggs

The Giggling Tree

"An egg?" said Ava. She was too excited to wait.

"How did you know?" demanded Oliver, showing her the egg he had hidden behind his back. It was exactly the same size and shape as Ava's,

but had purple speckles instead.

"Keep your voice down," whispered Ava.

"I guessed it was an egg because . . ."

She moved so that he could see her egg. "I found one, too!"

"Where do you think they came from?" Oliver breathed. He and Ava gently placed their eggs down side by side under the magnolia tree.

"Somewhere magical," said Ava. And it wasn't just because she always thought things were magical, either. Something about these eggs felt . . . different. *Special*. Like they were exactly what Ava had been waiting for.

The Giggling Tree

Oliver and Ava knelt down in front of the eggs and waited to see what they'd do next.

"This is so unbelievably cool," said Oliver, grinning from ear to ear. "Mystery eggs! In *our* backyard! Do you think we'll be on the news? But not one of the sad stories. I mean the part at the end, right before the weather, where they have a happy story to cheer everyone up. I'd like to be on that part. Ava? Ava, are you even listening?"

Mystery Eggs

Ava was staring at the egg, wondering dreamily when she'd last been this excited. On their last family vacation, probably. Or maybe on her eighth birthday, when they'd gone to the ice rink and then for ice cream. That had been really special, but it was *nowhere near* as amazing as this.

"Hello?" she whispered gently to her egg, hoping that it would do something, like wiggle or wobble or crack just a little. But nothing happened. Her smile wavered,

but she was convinced. These eggs
were magical. She just knew it.

"Hey!" said Oliver, leaning closer
to the mysterious egg. "Come out,
come out, whatever you are . . . ,"
he murmured, leaning so close that
his nose was almost touching his egg.
Nothing. **"Pfft,"** he said, sitting
back on his heels. "Whatever's inside,
it's boring!"

"Shhhhh!" said Ava. "You'll
hurt their feelings." Then she blinked.
Was she imagining it or had she just

seen two red eyes flash from inside Oliver's egg? She rubbed her eyes. The egg looked the same as it had before. Was she just seeing things?

"Sorry," said Oliver sheepishly.

A soft breeze blew, rustling the leaves of the magnolia tree and carrying Mom's words down the backyard. "Ava! Oliver! Lunch is ready!"

"We'd better go, Ollie," said Ava reluctantly. "They'll be wondering where we are."

The Giggling Tree

"Just one more minute," said Oliver, tapping his egg gently with a finger.

And that was when it happened.

Tat- a- tat.

Something inside the egg tapped back.

Rainbow Colors

"Lunch!" Mom's shout was so loud that Ava thought she could probably be heard in the next town. Ava looked at Oliver desperately, then back at the eggs. This was the very first time in her entire life that she'd found true, real-life magic. She couldn't leave her precious egg now, just to have *lunch*.

The Giggling Tree

"What if a fire-breathing dragon hatches out of the egg when we're not here?" Oliver asked.

"If you don't hurry," Dad's voice boomed, "I'm going to eat your lunch, too!"

A worried frown appeared on Oliver's forehead. "Actually," he said, "we should probably eat. I don't think it's a good idea to watch magic on an empty stomach."

Ava couldn't help laughing. Her brother's appetite was legendary.

"Come on," she said. "Let's hide the eggs somewhere warm and safe inside the house. Hopefully they won't do anything awesome while we're not watching!"

*

Lunch seemed to go on forever. Ava tried very hard to listen to Mom talk about her new passion for barbecuing, and Dad explain his latest bike, but all she could think about was getting back to her amazing mystery egg. Ava and Oliver gulped down their food and fidgeted until Mom and Dad said they could leave the table.

They ran straight to Ava's wardrobe, where they had hidden the eggs. Ava had decided that was the best spot for hatching. After all, the wardrobe was where the magic happened in Ava's favorite book, *The Lion, the Witch and the Wardrobe*. But *this* wardrobe didn't seem to be making any magic happen.

Ava carefully lifted her egg to rest on her knees. Oliver did the same with his.

"Maybe it's stuck?" Oliver said, after a few moments of silence. "Do you think I should crack my egg open? Just to help whatever it is get out, I mean."

"No!" Ava stared at her brother in horror. "How would you feel if you were in an egg and someone tried to crack it?"

Oliver clearly hadn't thought of it that way. "Well, maybe not, then," he said, looking at his egg again.

The air in the wardrobe was heavy

and silent. Ava shifted her hands to the base of her egg. It just felt right to hold it that way, somehow.

And then, very quietly . . .

Ba-dum. Ba-dum. Ba-dum.

The children gasped. A heartbeat!

"There really *is* something inside!" Ava breathed, awestruck.

"Ava . . . ," Oliver said. "Turn your egg around!"

"What? Why?" Ava was mesmerized by the sound of the little creature's heartbeat. She could feel it thudding gently underneath the egg's shell.

"Its eyes!" Oliver whispered.
"They're glowing through the egg!"

Wide-eyed, Ava spun her egg. Two large pink eyes shone through the velvety darkness. **"Whoa!"** she said.

Oliver began stroking and patting his egg, and tilted it from side to side. The creature inside went, **"Wheeee!"** Oliver's face lit up. "Mine has yellow eyes!" he cried, totally forgetting that they were supposed to be quiet.

"Wow!" cried Ava, who had forgotten about being quiet, too.

"How do you think we hatch it?" Oliver asked, as the creature inside his egg giggled. "I want to see what it is!"

Tat-a-tat.

He tried tapping his egg with one finger, just as he had in the backyard.

Tat-a-tat.

The creature inside tapped back!

Oliver beamed. "It's listening to me!" he exclaimed.

Ava thought hard. Ollie was right. Everything the eggs did seemed to be in answer to the children. So did that mean that they should be helping the eggs to hatch? And if so . . . how?

Oliver went back to tilting his egg, until suddenly its eyes turned green. The creature went, **"Bleurgh!"**

"I think it's feeling sick!" said Ava. She certainly would if someone was tilting *her* like that.

"Sorry, egg," said Oliver, rubbing it. "I didn't mean to make you feel sick."

His egg made a cooing sound.

"Let's take them back outside to where we found them," Ava decided. She was stiff from perching on old shoes on the floor of the wardrobe.

The Giggling Tree

Outside, the sun had vanished behind thick gray clouds, and the backyard was very chilly. Dad was inside loading the dishwasher, and Mom was banging tools around in the shed. They were way too busy to notice Ava and Oliver, who scurried to the farthest corner of the backyard, out of sight.

Still the eggs refused to hatch . . . but their eyes did turn a beautiful shade of pale blue. The color reminded Ava of something else. It was just like the sky on a frosty

The Giggling Tree

winter's morning, when lacy patterns
of ice decorated her bedroom window.

"I know!" Ava said. "They're *cold*."

The creature in Ava's egg made a
little shivery noise.

"So am I," Oliver said. He was
shivering, too. "I'm going to run

around the yard to warm up. Come
on, eggs. I'll take you with me."
He tucked them both inside his coat.

Ava watched nervously as Oliver
took off across the yard. Then he
zoomed back and skidded to a
stop, his cheeks red with the effort

of running. He pulled out his egg and rubbed it with both hands. The creature inside gave a contented sigh.

"At least its eyes aren't pale blue anymore," Oliver said uncertainly.

"No . . . ," said Ava, taking her egg back from him. "Now they're *dark* blue! Is it *scared*?"

"Oh no," wailed Oliver. "First I made it feel sick. Now I've scared my egg!"

Ava's egg had yellow eyes again

and was cooing gently, while Oliver's creature whimpered nervously from inside its egg.

"It's *never* going to hatch," Oliver said. "And I'm too excited to wait!"

"We just need to be patient," Ava said. "Will you let me give it a try? I think yours just needs a pat!"

Oliver passed Ava his egg. She patted it until it sighed and began to coo happily again. Ava smiled. But then she saw Oliver's expression—he looked as if his batteries had died.

"Cheer up, Ollie," she said softly.

"No," he replied, folding his arms.

Ava tried tickling him. That usually made him laugh. But Oliver just sat down and curled up into a ball.

"What do you call a monster with cheese in his ears?" Ava said.

"Dunno," muttered Oliver.

"Anything you want—it can't hear you!"

Oliver just rolled his eyes.

Ava thought hard. And then

suddenly, she knew how to make Oliver
feel better. She gave her brother a hug.

"Cut it out!" mumbled Oliver,
pushing her away.

But the hug had worked—now
he was smiling. Even better, it had
given Ava an idea. Hugs always made

everyone feel loved. So would hugs work with mystery eggs? Would that be enough to make them hatch? There was only one way to find out.

Ava picked up her egg and hugged it gently.

"Try it, Ollie," she said. "I think this just might work."

And as they hugged and hugged, the eggs' eyes started to flash the most wonderful rainbow colors! The creatures inside began to call out like little baby birds. Ava squealed with delight. Something magical was happening, she was sure of it. Maybe playing with the eggs had made them ready to hatch!

Who's Inside?

As Ava held her egg, a little beak began to **tat-a-tat** a hole in the shell.

Tat-a-tat. A second hole appeared. Then a third! Ava could hardly breathe, she was so excited. Soon they would find out who's inside!

The Giggling Tree

"Ollie," she said, "look!"

"Mine's doing it, too!" he gasped.

Slowly, slowly, the mystery creatures pecked hole after hole all around the eggs. Ava and Oliver rubbed the eggs to encourage them. Then . . . **crack!** A little beak broke through!

Eagerly, the two children began to peel away the pieces of eggshell to help the creatures hatch. At last— at long, long last—Ava managed to catch a glimpse of the creature inside.

Who's Inside?

At first, all she could see was bright pink fur. She stroked it gently and then the most adorable face she'd ever seen looked straight up at her.

The Giggling Tree

Fur the color of summer seas surrounded its huge eyes, which shone sunshine yellow. Its beak was pink. And on top of the creature's head was an adorable tuft of fuzzy purple fur.

"Hello there," Ava whispered. "Should I help you get out?"

The little creature wriggled in reply. Ava decided that meant "yes." So she reached her fingers inside the speckled egg and pulled the creature out of the broken shell. It made a low purring sound.

Who's Inside?

"You're beautiful!" murmured Ava. The animal sat in her cupped hands, just gazing at her. It was so furry, just like a koala. And now that it was fully hatched, she could see that the teal fur on its face covered its tummy, too!

Its purple feet reminded her of a penguin she'd seen at a wildlife sanctuary.

Perhaps most amazing of all, it had two tiny multicolored wings. They were purple and green and blue and pink.

"What should I call you?" she whispered. "You have wings and webbed feet like a penguin, but you're furry like a koala. I think you're a . . . Penguala!"

"Ava!" Oliver whispered.

Ava whirled around to see her brother carefully helping a purple creature wriggle out of its shell.

Who's Inside?

When she moved closer, she saw that it was very different from her Penguala.

"It's so cool!" Oliver said, beaming at Ava. He smoothed the creature's purple and white fur. He and Ava marveled at its blue beak and the spines on its back. Its wings were blue, too, with purple scales.

"What do you think it is?" Ava asked. She showed Oliver her creature, and explained that it was called a Penguala.

"Well," Oliver said, rubbing his chin in a serious fashion. "Mine is like a mini dragon," he said at last. "Look at the scales on its wings. See?"

Ava did see.

"But it has the face of an eagle," Oliver went on thoughtfully. "So that would make it . . . a Dragoneagle! Hmm. That doesn't sound right.

Who's Inside?

A Dragogle? A Drageagle? I know!
It's a Draggle."

"Perfect," said Ava, gently rubbing
the Penguala's tummy.

Suddenly the Penguala began to
sing a song made up of adorable coos.
It sounded like it was singing, *"Hatchy
birthday to me!"*

Ava was so
surprised that
she nearly
dropped her
Penguala.

The Giggling Tree

Oliver rubbed his Draggle's tummy, too, and at once it joined in with the birthday song.

"Yay!" cried Ava and Oliver. "It's their birthday!"

*

The only pets Ava and Oliver had ever owned before were two small goldfish. Oliver had named his Zzzzz, because he said the fish was so boring, it put him to sleep.

The Penguala and the Draggle were *nothing* like the goldfish.

Who's Inside?

On their first day after hatching, they needed a lot of looking after, like babies. But Ava and Oliver soon learned that the Penguala and Draggle used their eye colors to tell the children what they needed, just like they had from inside the eggs.

"Her eyes are purple, Ollie!" Ava called. "What does that color mean?!"

Oliver was on the sofa, tickling his Draggle. The little creature giggled and squirmed, flapping its wings with delight. "Maybe it's hungry?" he said.

The Giggling Tree

"But . . . what do you think Pengualas like to eat?" Ava asked.

She and Oliver paused in thought. The Draggle looked thoughtful, too— he always liked to copy Oliver.

"They have beaks like birds, and

birds eat worms," she mused.

Oliver grinned. "I've got just the thing!" he said, running off.

He returned a moment later with a bag of gummy worms. Ava looked doubtful.

"I'm not sure Pengualas like . . ." She trailed off. Her Penguala was wriggling wildly, its beak reaching for the gummy worms. Grinning back at Oliver, she tilted her Penguala so it could eat. It dug in, making adorable munching noises.

"We should keep them hidden,"
Ava said to Oliver, once her Penguala
had finished eating and curled up in
her lap. "Mom and Dad will freak out
if they see them."

Oliver wasn't so sure. "We could just
pretend they're toys," he said. "I bet
Mom and Dad won't suspect a thing."

To Ava's surprise, he was right.

"What are those funny little furry
things?" asked Mom when she saw
them.

"Just toys," Oliver said quickly.

Who's Inside?

"Mine is called Duke. Duke the Draggle! And Ava named hers Pippi, after the girl from that book she likes, *Pippi Longstocking.*"

The Giggling Tree

Ava held her breath, ready to admit everything and tell Mom that magic really did exist, and that the creatures had hatched from beautiful speckled eggs, and that if they had the hiccups, their eyes flashed orange, and—

"Great," said Mom. "Now, who wants to set the table?"

"Me!" said Ava and Oliver at once.

Phew! they mouthed at each other.

*

That night, the children fell asleep snuggled up with their new

Who's Inside?

furry friends. When Ava woke,
she wondered if she'd dreamed
her Penguala—but when a little
wing tickled her nose, she quickly
remembered the wonderful truth.

After that, Ava and Oliver spent
every possible moment looking after
Duke and Pippi.
The trickiest
thing was teaching
them to move
around.

"Like this, Pippi!"

Ava called, setting off down the hall at a run.

Pippi watched carefully from the other end of the hallway. She tried to copy Ava, but quickly tumbled over.

"Hmm." Ava helped Pippi up and gave her a cuddle. "Maybe we should start with walking, not running!"

Duke and Pippi got the hang of it eventually, but not until they'd joined wings and sung "Hatchy Birthday" again.

Who's Inside?

"Another birthday!" Oliver exclaimed.

"They must grow up faster than we do!" Ava said—then she and Oliver sang along with the creatures.

Now that Duke and Pippi knew how to walk, if the children didn't keep an eye on them, they vanished. And then anything could happen . . . like the time they jumped up and down on the remote control and changed the television channels all evening. Mom and Dad were very confused!

"Funny little creatures, aren't they?" said Dad. "What kind of batteries do they run on?"

"Um . . . I'm not sure," mumbled Ava, plucking up the Penguala and quickly taking her back to her room.

*

Who's Inside?

Meanwhile, Oliver was certain that Duke and Pippi were trying to tell them something. The Penguala and the Draggle would often scuttle to the window, look back at the children, and speak in their own secret language.

"What's up, Duke?" Oliver asked.

But the children couldn't understand Duke's answer.

Soon, with lots of practice, the Draggle and the Penguala could repeat words back to the children. **"Hello!"** they would call when they woke up, looking very proud of themselves. Ava and Oliver even taught them how to dance—once they'd gotten the hang of walking. But they *still* couldn't speak well enough to explain why they kept running to the window.

Who's Inside?

And then, finally, they had another birthday—and could speak at last!

"The tree needs us!" called Pippi and Duke, heading for the back door.

Wide-eyed and breathless, Ava and Oliver followed them out into the backyard. The creatures were zooming toward the magnolia tree, where Ava had found Pippi.

"They must mean this tree," said Ava.

"Tat-a-tat!" said the little creatures. **"Tat-a-tat!"**

The Giggling Tree

"Ollie, I've got it!" Ava exclaimed. "That was the tapping sound they made when they were hatching.

Who's Inside?

Remember? They want us to tap again—"

"On the tree!" finished Oliver.

So, trembling with excitement, the two children slowly began to tap on the trunk of the tree.

Tat- a- tat.

Tat- a- tat.

Tat- a- tat!

Through the Door

Creak . . .

They could barely hear it at first.

Creak . . .

Then it grew louder and louder.

Creak . . .

At last the children knew what the sound was. A door was creaking open in the tree trunk!

The Giggling Tree

Ava hopped around with excitement as the faintest outline appeared, and a rectangle of pale light glowed there.

It was a door, but unlike any Ava had ever seen. To begin with, it was very, very small—so small that it only came up to Ava's knee. There was no handle. It seemed that the only way to open this door was to tap on the tree. Though how anyone would know it was there in the first place was a mystery, because the door was perfectly camouflaged. Its surface was the rough, knobby tree trunk.

"Wow," whispered Oliver, crouching down for a closer look.

The Giggling Tree

"Check out Pippi and Duke," Ava whispered, joining him.

The Penguala and the Draggle were spinning each other around and laughing gleefully.

"This is obviously what they wanted us to find!" Oliver said, beaming.

The door's outline began to gleam more brightly. The children held their breath as the door opened fully . . . to reveal a sight so beautiful that it dazzled their eyes. It was all colors of the rainbow, from ruby red to

Through the Door

darkest violet—and every shade in between. If Ava squinted against the glow, she could just about see a world in miniature: bright blue sky, rolling white clouds, and lush green grass scattered with flowers of every color.

"If only we could see more . . . ," Ava sighed. The doorway was so small that it was impossible to catch more than a glimpse of the amazing place beyond.

But the doorway was just the right size for a Penguala and a Draggle.

The Giggling Tree

As Ava and Oliver watched, their new friends skipped through it. Then they stopped and looked back.

"Follow us!" called the two creatures. Ava could have cried with frustration. The magical world was close enough to touch, but they'd

Through the Door

never be able to get there. "I wish we could," she said sadly, "but we're too big."

Pippi gave a tinkling laugh. "This way!" she said.

"The tree needs us!" added Duke.

Ava reached down and wiggled her

hand through the doorway, wishing desperately that she could squeeze the rest of her body through into the other world. But then the strangest thing happened. As soon as she poked her fingers through the doorway, the opening seemed to grow. She stumbled forward, and then the other world grew, too. Best of all, so did her Penguala. Now Pippi wasn't the size of a kitten. She came up to Ava's waist!

"Now that we're nearly the same

size, I can finally cuddle you back!"
Pippi said, and pulled Ava in for a hug.

Ava laughed and squeezed her
friend tight. It was strange hearing
Pippi talk—she was all grown up
now! Then Ava turned back to Oliver
and nearly fell over with amazement.
Her brother looked like a giant on
the other side of the doorway! His
goggling eyes were as big as goldfish
bowls. His hands were the same size as
Ava. She could see right up his nose,
and she tried not to laugh.

Through the Door

"Whoa!" she said, and then suddenly she understood.

The world through the doorway hadn't grown. Ava had shrunk!

"You're tiny!" Oliver exclaimed, gawking down at his sister. "How did you do that?"

Ava stepped back a little. "Try putting your hand through!"

Oliver, who could hardly hear his sister now that she was so small, leaned down to poke his head through the doorway.

The Giggling Tree

Then Oliver promptly shrank.

"Phew!" said Ava. She wouldn't

have wanted to go without him.

Her brother stared down at his

hands, back up at Ava, and then out at the amazing, multicolored world around them. "I think we've found the magic you've been looking for!" he said.

The Giggling Tree

It was better than Ava could have imagined. Bluebells tinkled merrily like real bells. Sunflowers really did shine. And, beyond the lush, tall trees around them, Ava could see hazy blue mountains reaching into the cottony clouds. It was as if everything had been dipped in the brightest paint and sprinkled with glitter.

"Hurray!" cried a singsong voice. "You brought help!"

Ava dragged her eyes away from the dazzling view to see that they didn't just have Duke and Pippi for company. There was a whole crowd of amazing creatures waiting for them.

"Whoa!" cried Oliver.

A creature with orange and black stripes glided toward them. He reminded Ava of a tiger, but with silvery wings and a feathered blue tummy.

"I'm Tigrette," he said, his voice as loud and clear as a bell. "Welcome to Hatchtopia, the Hatchimals' world!"

"*What*-chimals?" asked Oliver.

The Giggling Tree

"What did you say?"

"Hatchimals," repeated Tigrette, smiling warmly. "Didn't you know? We're all Hatchimals." He gestured to the creatures crowded behind him.

"Hatchimals," Ava whispered. The name was perfect. "I'm Ava, and this is Ollie. It's great to meet you. But can I ask, umm . . . Why are we here?"

"To save the tree, of course!" said Tigrette. He pointed behind the children with one paw.

Ava and Oliver turned around . . .

and stared at an amazing, beautiful, *enormous* tree. In its trunk was a familiar-looking doorway.

"Wait," said Ava. "Did we just come through this tree? But . . . where did the magnolia tree from our backyard go?"

"It's still in your yard," Tigrette said. "One side of the door is in your magnolia tree. The other side of the door is in *this* tree: the Giggling Tree."

The Giggling Tree was huge. Its roots sprawled like gigantic feet. The trunk was solid and sturdy. Branches soared upward and outward, hung with many tiny leaves. But the things that made the tree so special were the tiny flickers of light that sparkled and shone from its leaves, and glittered like fireflies in the air around it.

"It's a magical tree that spreads laughter and cheer," Tigrette told them, looking up at the tree proudly. "When you're near it, you *always* feel happy!"

The Giggling Tree

So why did Ava suddenly feel so much like crying? She blinked. Had she imagined it, or were the tiny flickers disappearing, one by one? She kept watching. They were. *Oh dear.* That couldn't be good.

Tigrette hung his head. "There's something wrong with our beloved tree," he said sadly. "We don't know what it is, and we don't know how to fix it. All we know is that the Giggling Tree has stopped laughing."

"The tree laughs?" Oliver asked.

Through the Door

"Yes." A bright pink creature cantered forward to join Tigrette. It shook its orange mane and tail. "I'm Ponette," it said, with a small bow. "The Giggling Tree has always laughed . . . until now. It's stopped. And that's very, very bad news."

"Why?" asked Ava.

The Giggling Tree

"The Giggling Tree is the source of all seeds in Hatchtopia," explained Pippi, stepping forward. "Without it, no more trees can grow here. Look, you can see how sick the tree is. Its sparkles are starting to go out!"

Ava felt a small tear trickle down her cheek. She looked around at the beautiful world and tried to imagine it without trees—and couldn't.

"It gets worse," added Tigrette. "Without new trees, new Hatchimals will have nowhere to nest."

Through the Door

Ava looked around again. Now that she knew what to look for, she could spot lots of eggs nestled in the trees and tucked in their roots.

Some braver Hatchimals had fluttered closer to get a good look at the visitors. They darted between the flowers, their wings sparkling. Every single Hatchimal was so special. Ava couldn't stand the idea of them having nowhere to nest.

"Okay," she said briskly, "let's hatch a plan!"

Hatching a Plan

"The poor Giggling Tree," said Ava, gazing up at its drooping leaves. "I wonder why it isn't giggling anymore?"

"Maybe it's unhappy," said Oliver. "I never feel like laughing when I'm sad."

The Hatchimals nodded to one

another, murmuring softly.

"So we need to cheer it up," said Ava.

"Yes, but how?" asked Oliver. "How do we make a tree laugh? In our world, trees don't laugh. They don't even smile. They just rustle a bit and wave in the wind. So how can we know what this tree thinks is funny?"

"Umm," said Ava. She hadn't gotten that far yet, and now Oliver and all the Hatchimals were staring at her, which made it really difficult to think of a clever plan. "Well, what makes *you* laugh?" she finally asked.

"Oh, *lots* of things," said Oliver. He bounced up and down as he described his favorite funny things. "I love it when a custard pie splats someone in the face. And people falling over is hilarious, especially when they fall into kiddie pools. Oh, and remember that time I fooled you into putting salt on your cereal instead of sugar, Ava? The face you pulled was awesome. And that made *you* laugh, too!"

Pippi and Duke looked at each

other in horror. It didn't seem like they thought any of those things were funny.

"Okay . . . Thanks, Ollie," said Ava.

"I'll try the falling-over thing now," said Oliver brightly.

Before Ava could stop him, he was strolling past the Giggling Tree, whistling a chirpy tune. "Oops!" he cried, pretending to trip over a tree root. He dived onto the ground, where he performed a neat forward roll and sprang to his feet again, with a loud **"Ta-daaaaaaa!"**

Everyone turned to the Giggling Tree. They all waited nervously.

There was nothing, not even a rustle of the tiniest leaf.

"Well, it looks like *that* didn't work," Oliver said. "Too bad. That was one of my best dives ever."

The Giggling Tree

Ava frowned. It seemed like this was going to be more difficult than she'd thought. She so wanted to be able to help the Hatchimals. Duke and Pippi had been so sure that Ava and Oliver would be able to do something. Ava hated the thought of letting her new friends down.

"You'll think of something, won't you?" said Pippi hopefully. Ava stroked the Penguala's soft fur.

"We'll try our very best," she replied.

"I know!" said Oliver, clapping his hands. "Let's blow raspberries!"

So Ava, Oliver, and the Hatchimals blew raspberries at the Giggling Tree until they were laughing so hard, they thought they might pop.

Sadly, the Giggling Tree wasn't laughing with them.

"How about we tell jokes?" suggested Ava. "I'll go first!" She turned toward the Giggling Tree. "What did the tree wear to the pool party?"

The Giggling Tree didn't reply.

"Swimming trunks!" said Ava. She and Pippi burst into giggles.

Not even the tiniest chuckle came from the Giggling Tree.

It didn't laugh when they pulled faces, either—not even when Tigrette twisted his ears to make his tongue poke out. Oh dear. This wasn't good. And the Hatchimals were starting to look really worried.

"I know. Let's try tickling the tree," Ava suggested, determined not to give up.

Hatching a Plan

"That always makes me laugh."

"Great idea!" said Oliver. "I wonder if its feet are as ticklish as mine are."

"Can we help?" asked a blue Hatchimal who looked like an elephant. "I'm Elefly. I'm good at tickling!"

"Oh, yes, please join in," said Ava, smiling gratefully. It was clear that they needed all the help they could get.

Elefly beckoned the other Hatchimals over and introduced them. First came Kittycan, who looked like

a cross between a furry kitten and
a toucan. She was sunflower yellow,
with a blue tummy and big dark eyes.
Koalabee came next, with green-blue
fur and a purple tummy and ears. He
smiled, but was too shy to speak. Both
had silvery wings like the others.

Next there was Girreo, then Puppit,
then Swotter, then Bunwee . . .
There were so many amazing new
Hatchimals that Ava couldn't keep
up. She crossed her fingers tightly and
wished hard that she'd have the chance

to get to know them better.

"Is everyone ready?" Oliver asked, as the furry creatures gathered around the Giggling Tree, shuffling for space.

There was a sea of nods.

"Then it's time for Operation Giggle!" cried Oliver. "Ready . . . set . . . tickle!"

It was so much fun! Ava tickled high and low. Oliver tickled every tiny branch that he could reach. The Hatchimals tickled everywhere in between.

Hatching a Plan

Ava held her breath. Surely this would work. It *had* to work. Any second now, the Giggling Tree would be laughing, Hatchtopia would be safe, and Pippi, Duke, Tigrette, and all the other Hatchimals would be so happy! Any second now . . .

Was that a flicker? A glimmer? Were the Giggling Tree's firefly lights getting any brighter?

Maybe a *little*. But its leaves were still curled and brown at the edges, and the branches still looked limp.

The Giggling Tree

"Stop!" shouted Oliver at last, his shoulders drooping like the tree's leaves. "I don't think this is working. It helped a little, but we need to try something else."

Meanwhile, the Hatchimals were so nervous that their huge eyes had darkened until they were deepest blue.

"What can we do?" wailed Pippi.

Duke began to sniffle sadly.

Hatching a Plan

Slumping to the ground with a miserable sigh, Ava gazed around at the enchanting home of the Hatchimals.

Nearby, a dainty wooden bridge crossed a shining stream. On the far side was a garden that sparkled and dazzled. Everything glittered—the grass, the trees, even the winding path. Brightly speckled eggs dotted the scene, nestled in among flowers and branches.

A sob rose at the back of Ava's throat. What if no more trees would grow in Hatchtopia?

"Umm," Oliver said quietly, "there is one more thing that might cheer up the Giggling Tree. It's something that made me feel happier."

He kicked a stone and looked so awkward that Ava wondered what he was going to say.

Hatching a Plan

"What is it?" she whispered. "Quick. There's no time to lose."

"A hug," muttered Oliver under his breath. "When I was feeling sad because I couldn't hatch Duke's egg, you gave me a hug, and that's what made me feel better. I think that might be what the Giggling Tree needs, too."

It was so amazingly simple that Ava burst out laughing.

"Don't laugh at me!" Oliver said.

"I'm not!" said Ava quickly. "I'd never laugh at you for that, Ollie. Everyone

needs a hug sometimes. I'm laughing because it's such a clever idea!"

"Oh," said Oliver, brightening. "That's okay, then."

Ava explained the plan to the curious Hatchimals crowded around them.

"Ooooh," chorused the Hatchimals, their dark blue eyes immediately changing to bright pink. "We like it!"

"But we must hurry," Tigrette said firmly. "The Giggling Tree is fading fast. We don't have much time!"

"Right," said Ava. "Could everyone please form a huge circle around the tree trunk?"

Once again, everyone leaped and flew into position, the Hatchimals' pink eyes shining like twinkle lights. The children crossed their fingers and wished hard.

"Ready . . . ," said Ava.

"Set . . . ," said Oliver.

"Squeeeeeeeeeeze!" said all of the Hatchimals together.

A Very Special Sound

Ava, Oliver, and the Hatchimals
wrapped their arms and their paws and
their wings around the Giggling Tree
and hugged for all they were worth.

It was the best group hug *ever*.

"Hatchimals are really good at
hugging," Duke whispered proudly,
"but this is a Hatchimal hug and a half.

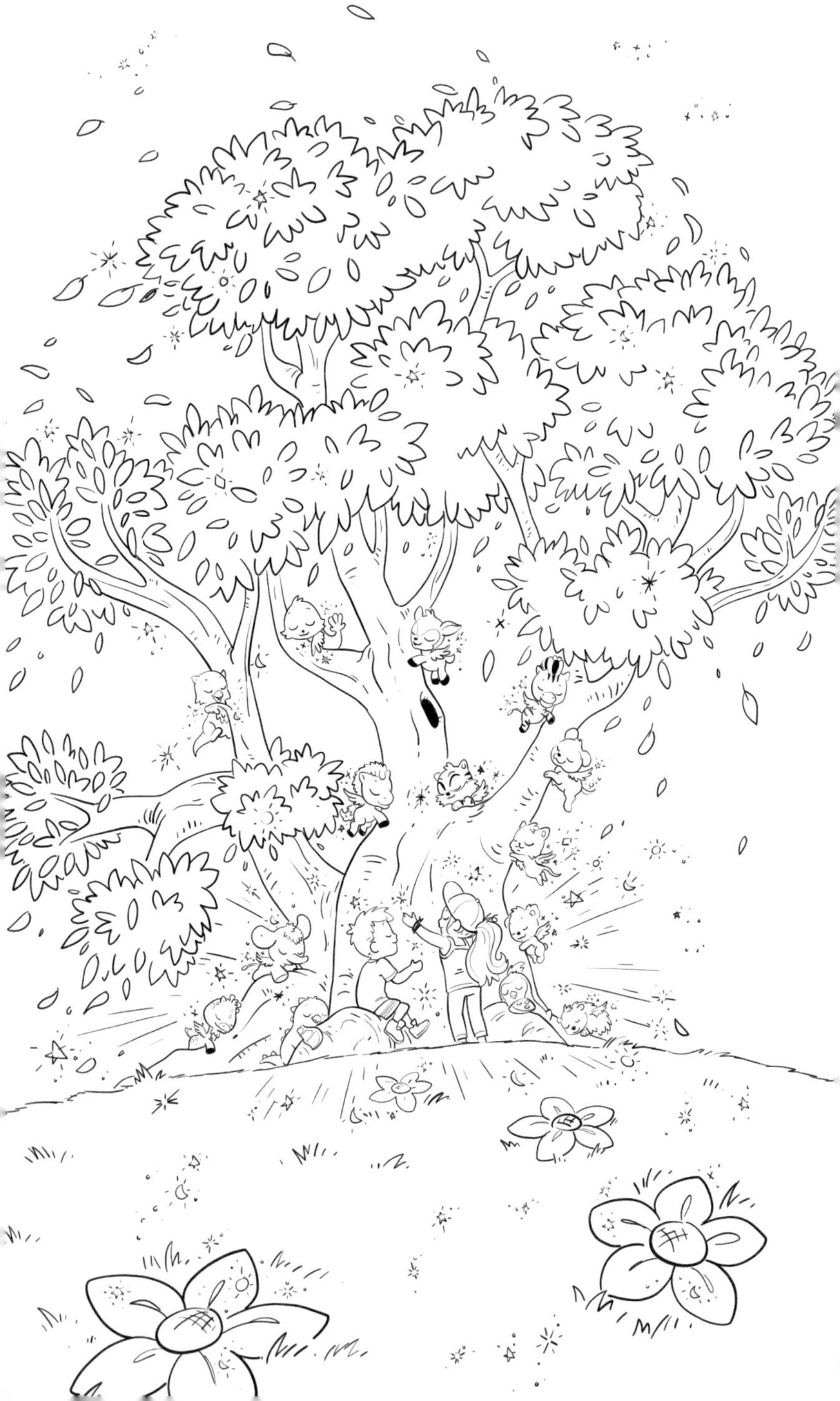

A Very Special Sound

If this doesn't make the Giggling Tree feel better, nothing will!"

Ava had to agree. New friends and old friends had joined together, and the air was filled with love and friendship.

The question was . . . would the hug actually work?

"Hee!"

The sound was so light and airy that only the Hatchimals in the highest branches could hear it at first. Everyone hugged tighter and tighter, until . . .

"Hee hee!"

"I'm sure I heard something," Oliver whispered.

Ava had heard it, too. Could it be . . . ?

"Hee hee hee! Ha ha hee! Hee ha hee!"

It was!

"The Giggling Tree is giggling again!" cried Ava. "We did it!"

"Yay!" Oliver let go of the tree to run in delighted circles around its trunk.

A Very Special Sound

The tiny giggles reminded Ava of a bubbling fountain. They started low down in the tree's enormous roots, before rushing up the wide, strong trunk, and then spraying upward and outward until the tree was shaking with laughter.

"Look," breathed Ava, taking a few steps backward so she could see the whole magnificent tree.

The others did the same, gazing up at the Giggling Tree in awe. The tree was changing before their eyes.

The Giggling Tree

One by one, the sad, drooping
leaves were flooding with color—
a bright emerald green that made the
brown, crispy edges vanish at once,
leaving behind leaves that were so
glossy and green that they looked
brand-new.

"Wow," said Oliver. "It's like . . ."

"Magic," Ava finished for him. "It's like magic."

And it really was. Here was the very thing that Ava had been searching for, right here in the enchanting world of Hatchtopia. She was so overjoyed, she wondered if she might even be happier than the Giggling Tree, which was still chuckling merrily to itself.

"Hee hee hee! Ha ha ha! Ha ha hee! Ha ha ha! Ha ha hee!"

With a whoosh of sparkles, the

tree's leaves began to twinkle again. But unlike before, when it had been a half-hearted flickering, now the tree actually glittered all over with light.

"It's *so* cool!" Oliver sighed. "Hey, do you think if we hug all the trees in our world, they might light up like this? Because that would be *amazing*."

Ava grinned. "We could try, and see what happens," she said. Then she froze, because tiny, tiny specks of light were now sailing through the air, flipping and floating in the sunlight.

Oh no. Had the magic stopped working? Was the Giggling Tree shedding its sparkles?

"What's happening?" said Ava, her lip trembling.

The Hatchimals laughed gently.

"Don't worry," said Tigrette, his voice deep and comforting. "It means that the Giggling Tree's magic is working." He held out a paw and caught one of the silvery sparkles, which he showed to Ava and Oliver. "Look closely," he said.

A Very Special Sound

"Wow!" said Ava as she peered at the teardrop-shaped speck on the Hatchimal's paw. "It's beautiful."

The little sparkle was a pale silvery-green color, and patterns seemed to dance on its surface.

"This is a magical seed from the Giggling Tree," explained Tigrette. "Wherever it lands, it will grow into a brand-new tree, where Hatchimal eggs can nest."

"Our world is safe!" said Pippi, spinning around with delight. "Ava and

Oliver healed the Giggling Tree! I *knew* you could do it," she told her friends.

"Hee hee hee! Ha ha ha! Ha ha hee! Hee hee ha! Ha ha heeee!" giggled the tree, as if to prove it.

"Hurray!" cheered Ava, relaxing at last. Finally it really did seem that everything would be all right in Hatchtopia. She hugged Pippi and

Duke, and then turned
to Oliver.

Oliver took a step
backward. "That's
enough hugging for
me," he said firmly.
"I'm saving mine in
case anything else
around here needs to be cheered up."

"How about a hatch five, then?"
Duke suggested, raising one wing to
show Oliver how to do it. "It's a high
five, but for Hatchimals!"

"Perfect!" Ava said, grinning and hatch-fiving her brother.

Duke and Pippi hatch-fived them, too. The other Hatchimals fluttered up into the sky and cheered.

"We can't thank you enough for all your help!" said Pippi.

Duke nodded. "And it's been so much fun having you in our world," he said.

Ava gulped. The Hatchimals were saying goodbye. She felt a rush of sadness. Of course . . . The Penguala and the Draggle had been sent to their world for a reason. The Hatchimals had needed their help. Now that the Giggling Tree was all better, there was no reason for Ava and Oliver to stay.

Ava swallowed hard and tried to be brave. "We've enjoyed every minute," she told Pippi and Duke.

"Well, other than the part when we thought we couldn't cheer up the tree," said Oliver. "That wasn't great." He gave a grin that stretched almost from ear to ear. "But the rest was *awesome*. Is the whole world as cool as this?"

Duke laughed. "Of course!" he said. "You're right, Giggle Grove is wonderful, but there's so much more to see. Like Lilac Lake, where you can swim in the purple water. Or Polar Paradise, where it's always snowy. Or Crystal Canyon, which is made of gemstones and jewels."

"Could this place *get* any better?" said Oliver. "Oh, hang on. I think it just did. Look at *that*." He peered into the distance, and Ava followed his gaze.

Wow. Just wow. How had she

A Very Special Sound

missed that? There, in the sapphire-blue sky, was a floating island made entirely of fluffy white clouds. But that wasn't even the best part. At the very heart of the clouds was a waterfall—a huge glassy curtain of water that poured down to earth, twinkling with stars.

"Ah, that's Wishing Star Waterfall," said Duke. "Can you see where it begins, high up in Cloud Cove?"

Ava and Oliver nodded wordlessly.

"There's so much more to see here," Duke went on. "But . . ."

"We understand," said Ava. "It's time to go."

"It's been awesome," Oliver told them. "Come and visit us in our world sometime. Maybe you can teach us how to fly!"

"What do you mean?" asked Pippi, as the brother and sister circled the Giggling Tree, looking for the way out.

A Very Special Sound

"Where are you going?"

"Er . . . home?" Oliver looked puzzled.

"What, without us?" said Pippi.

"What did you say?" whispered Ava, hope fluttering in her tummy.

"Wait for us!" said Duke. "You helped us to hatch, so we're *your* Hatchimals now. You can't get rid of us that easily."

"Really?" Oliver gasped. "You're coming back with us?"

"And this isn't goodbye?" said Ava.

Pippi and Duke looked at each other and smiled. "Of course not," they chorused. "Come on! Let's go."

Ava felt giggles bubbling up inside her. She knew exactly how the Giggling Tree had felt. She and Oliver had finally found true, real-life magic. There was a whole new world to explore.

And, best of all, they had Duke the Draggle and Pippi the Penguala to explore it with them.

THE END

Hatchimals come from different families. Orange Tigrette is from the Jungle family, and Pink Ponette is from the Farm family! Some Hatchimal family names are listed below. Can you find them in this word search?

G	G	R	J	F	A	R	M	X	M
A	L	O	C	E	A	N	S	V	F
R	S	B	B	K	W	E	J	I	O
D	L	A	C	M	R	X	U	P	R
E	Q	B	V	E	J	K	N	W	E
N	X	M	V	A	G	U	G	O	S
A	W	I	Y	D	N	W	L	R	T
Y	R	Z	N	O	K	N	E	M	A
X	V	F	Y	W	H	P	A	Q	O
W	X	D	E	S	E	R	T	H	H

RIVER   OCEAN   JUNGLE

FARM   FOREST   SAVANNAH

DESERT   GARDEN   MEADOW

The Hatchimals Ava meets remind her of animals in our world. Can you try crossing two animals together, and see what kind of creature you might get?

Choose two animals from the list, and then draw your new Hatchimal here!

eagle	seagull	parrot	fish	deer
cat	badger	donkey	hamster	dove
squirrel	horse	bear	penguin	dog
rhino	magpie	wren	fox	lizard

Word search answer

C	G	R	J	F	A	R	M	X	M
A	L	O	C	E	A	N	S	V	F
P	S	B	B	K	W	E	J	I	O
D	L	A	C	M	R	X	U	P	R
E	Q	B	V	I	J	K	N	W	E
N	X	M	A	G	U	G	O	S	
A	W	Y	D	N	W	L	R		
Y	R	Z	N	O	K	E	M	A	
X	V	F	Y	W	H	P	A	Q	O
W	X	D	E	S	E	R	T	H	H

Also available

LILAC SWHALE

This Hatchimal nests in the Violet Vines of Lilac Lake.

FAMILY: LILAC LAKE
RARITY: RARE
FLIGHT ABILITY: 2/5

GIGGLING PANDOR

This giggly little Pandor is super sweet and loves to cuddle.

FAMILY: GIGGLE GROVE
RARITY: COMMON
FLIGHT ABILITY: 3/5

PINK CHIPADEE

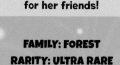

Pink Chipadee is really musical—she loves to play for her friends!

FAMILY: FOREST
RARITY: ULTRA RARE
FLIGHT ABILITY: 4/5

PINK LEORIOLE

Pink Leoriole has a very loud roar!

FAMILY: SAVANNAH
RARITY: COMMON
FLIGHT ABILITY: 2/5

HOLD! HATCH! PLAY!

HOLD! HATCH! PLAY!

HATCHIMALS™ & © Spin Master Ltd., used under license.

HATCHIMALS™ & © Spin Master Ltd., used under license.

HOLD! HATCH! PLAY!

HOLD! HATCH! PLAY!

HATCHIMALS™ & © Spin Master Ltd., used under license.

HATCHIMALS™ & © Spin Master Ltd., used under license.